Earth to Audrey

✳

For Jennifer Meeker, my dear sister — S.H.

To Courtney and Louise — S.P.

✳

Kids Can Press acknowledges the financial support of the
Government of Ontario, through the Ontario Media Development
Corporation's Ontario Book Initiative; the Ontario Arts Council;
the Canada Council for the Arts; and the Government of Canada,
through the BPIDP, for our publishing activity.

Published in Canada by
Kids Can Press Ltd.
29 Birch Avenue
Toronto, ON M4V 1E2

Published in the U.S. by
Kids Can Press Ltd.
2250 Military Road
Tonawanda, NY 14150

www.kidscanpress.com

The artwork in this book was rendered in oil on canvas.
The text is set in Berkeley.

Edited by Tara Walker
Designed by Karen Powers

Printed and bound in China

This book is smyth sewn casebound.

CM 05 0 9 8 7 6 5 4 3 2 1

Library and Archives Canada Cataloguing in Publication

Hughes, Susan, 1960–
    Earth to Audrey / written by Susan Hughes ;
illustrated by Stéphane Poulin.

ISBN 1-55337-843-1

I. Poulin, Stéphane II. Title.

PS8565.U42E27 2005   jC813'.6   C2005-900280-8

Kids Can Press is a Corus™ Entertainment company

Earth to Audrey

Written by Susan Hughes

Illustrated by Stéphane Poulin

Kids Can Press

The first time I saw Audrey, I almost didn't.

The next time I saw her, she was sending signals. There couldn't have been anyone up there answering back ... could there?

When I saw Audrey again, she was training grasshoppers. Her antennae had to be fake. But the grasshoppers didn't seem to think so.

After that, I kept my eyes peeled for Audrey. I never knew where she would turn up. I never knew what she might be doing. She might be creating a strange concoction. She might be building an odd contraption. Lots of times, she was just lying down looking up.

I began to wonder. Was she from another planet? Was she an alien?

Summer holidays had already begun. The neighborhood was quiet. My friends, Sam and Ahmed, were away at camp. So I decided. Audrey had to be an alien. I had always wanted to meet an alien, and my friends would want me to meet one too. That's why, when I saw Audrey again, I stopped my bike.

"What do you want?" Audrey said. I could tell she hadn't learned many Earth manners yet.

"My name is Ray," I answered. She didn't speak. "Why do you lie down so much?" I asked, trying to keep my voice friendly. Maybe she had a laser gun, or a spaceship hovering nearby with a tractor beam to haul me aboard.

Audrey paused. Then she shrugged. "Try it for yourself," she suggested.

No sign of a laser gun or a tractor beam,
so I cartwheeled over and lay down beside her.

The wind blew. The green leaves swayed
and waved.

"Green, green, green," said Audrey.
She sounded like she was talking to
herself. Or to someone who wasn't there.
"How can one small word be big enough
to describe all this?"

I wondered too. And I was the
one who lived here on this planet.

The next time I saw Audrey, she was taking
off her shoes and socks. She saw me, but she
didn't say anything. Still no Earth manners.

I went over and took off my shoes and
socks too. We stretched out our arms and legs,
starfish-like.

"I can feel the Earth holding me," Audrey
said, smiling.

"Me too," I said, surprised.

Audrey rolled over and pressed her cheek
against the hot grass. She hugged the Earth back.

I took her over to the
sandpit a few days later.
"My name is Audrey. I'm
staying with my father for
the summer," she explained.
It had taken her a long time to
come up with that story. I nodded as
if I believed her. I wondered what her
true alien name was. Audrey buried me,
all except my head. Another Earth hug.

It was fun getting to know an alien. I never
knew what to expect. Sometimes I would
tell Audrey something and she wouldn't
hear me. Was she communicating with
someone from her home planet?
   "Earth to Audrey! Earth to Audrey!"
I'd call, and she'd laugh.

By the middle of the summer, Audrey was more comfortable speaking Earth English. She talked to me more.

"Hey, Ray. I want to show you something that I brought from home," Audrey said.

Her spaceship? Some galactic dust? Some plasma pets?

"On Earth, it's simple. Up is here, and down is here," Audrey said, holding a globe and pointing. "But when you're in space, maybe this is up — or *this*." She turned the globe upside down, then sideways.

I felt like we were in her spaceship, seeing the Earth for the first time, new and astonishing.

Audrey's brother, Timothy, arrived from basketball camp one hot afternoon. He crossed his eyes. He snapped his gum. He didn't say hello.

Then, ta-da! There was a basketball spinning on his finger.

"Ha!" Audrey laughed. "Imagine it's the Earth, spinning once around for each day."

"But what started the Earth spinning?" I wondered.

"And why?" she whispered.

The ball twirled forever as we watched. Days and months and years passed. Aliens can make you see the future.

The next day Audrey said, "Hey, Ray. Let's go for
an Earth ride."

Aliens are patient. We sat still for a long time,
trying to feel the Earth move.

Slowly, the Earth rolled us out of the shadows and
into the sunshine. We wiggled the tips of our toes.

Then I grabbed onto the grass and shouted to
the Earth, "You are a leaping dolphin, and we are
on your back!"

Audrey yelled, "We are along for the ride, and we
won't fall off!"

I stopped looking at the calendar. I wasn't missing Sam and Ahmed. I wanted summer to last forever.

I invited Audrey for picnics in the park. I showed her how to ride bikes around the track, pretending we were horses. She showed me how to find the North Star and the Big Dipper.

I took Audrey to swim at the public pool. After watching her in the water, I could tell there weren't swimming pools on her planet.

Audrey took me to see a movie, *The Creature That Came from Beyond!* She said she was disappointed. She didn't think the creature was very realistic.

Then August was ending. The sky seemed far away. Audrey's planet must be even farther away, I thought. I couldn't imagine so much space between us.

The night her mother arrived, Audrey invited me over. She didn't have to tell me. I knew she would be leaving soon.

When I got there, everyone was lying on the lawn, joined at the head like an earthbound star.

"Hey, Ray," Audrey whispered in the dark, making room.

"BANG!" said Audrey's mother suddenly. I jumped, and Audrey took my hand. "There was nothing at all, and then, bang! The universe began. Suddenly there was something. The first something. An explosion of stuff," she explained.

I remembered before meeting Audrey and then after meeting Audrey. Nothing and then something.

"Everything comes from that beginning," Audrey's mother went on. "Everything comes from the very first particles created in that first explosion — the bits and pieces that make up the trees, the animals, the water, each one of us, all the people who have ever been, the Earth, the other planets, the stars, everything in all the other hundred billion galaxies and everything in between. Everything that ever was and everything that ever will be comes from that great explosion at the very beginning."

Into the silence, I asked hopefully, "Even aliens?"

"Even aliens," Audrey's mother agreed. "Everything shares a first home."

We lay, looking up and feeling close, for a long time.

The next day was the last day. I wondered if Audrey might give up her life in space. Earth was a good place to live. I could see that she was getting to like it.

"Maybe you could stay," I suggested to her. "Maybe you could live here instead."

She didn't answer right away, but I waited. I knew her Earth manners had improved.

"I can't stay, but I'll come back next summer," Audrey promised. "I wouldn't miss it for anything in the whole universe."

And so I'm going to keep my eyes peeled for Audrey. Who knows where she'll turn up? Who knows what she might be doing? I don't want to miss her.